SCRUFFY
The Scamp

Home Farm Twins

Scruffy
The Scamp

Jenny Oldfield

Illustrated by Kate Aldous

Hodder
Children's
Books

a division of Hodder Headline plc

A Catalogue record for this book is available from the British Library

ISBN 0 340 70399 7

Typeset by Avon Dataset Ltd, Bidford-on-Avon, Warks

Printed and bound in Great Britain by
Mackays, Chatham, Kent

Hodder Children's Books
a division of Hodder Headline plc
338 Euston Road
London NW1 3BH

One

'I have to sing a solo!' Helen Moore wailed.

'When?' Her dad hung holly and mistletoe from the ceiling of the Curlew Cafe. He wobbled at the top of his stepladder while the rest of the family told him off for putting the bunches in the wrong places.

'Next week. At the Christmas concert. And I can't even sing!' Helen was dreading having to stand up in front of all her friends at her small village school.

'You can say that again!' Her twin sister, Hannah laughed out loud. 'Move that bunch to

1

the right a bit, Dad. Now down a bit, left a bit, up a bit . . . !'

'Who asked you?' Helen shoved Hannah out of the way. It was her job to clean the cafe floor, ready for the big Christmas party. All their friends from Doveton and their regular cafe customers in Nesfield had been invited. 'Anyway, I've been having nightmares about it!'

'I think you have a nice voice!' Mary Moore protested, coming in from the kitchen with a pile of clean white tablecloths.

'That's because you're my mum,' Helen grunted. She slopped the mop over the tiled floor. Soapy water splashed everywhere.

'Squeeze it out a bit more.' Mrs Moore took it from her. 'Like this. Now, Helen, if you're not going to do a job properly, it would be better to make yourself scarce.'

'She's sulking because she has to sing The Twelve Days of Christmas!' Hannah gloated. She stepped back into the puddle and slipped. 'Aagh!' Down on her backside.

It was Helen's turn to laugh. Speckle, their dog, rushed up to Hannah thinking she wanted to play.

'*Gerroff*, Speckle!' Hannah's dark, straight hair fell across her face, the seat of her jeans was wet. She began to wrestle with the dog. 'I'm not kidding! Let me get up!'

Speckle bounced all over her.

'Will someone tell me if I've got this holly straight!' David Moore demanded from the top of the wobbly ladder.

'All right, everyone, that's enough!' Mrs Moore put up her hands in surrender. 'We have to be ready for this party in two hours' time and I can't even hear myself think!'

'No one can *hear* themselves think!' Helen pointed out. She hauled Hannah to her feet and pushed Speckle away.

Her mother ignored her. She listed the things they still had to do. 'I have to bake a hundred mince-pies, two dozen sausage-rolls, and a carrot-cake. We have to set the tables with the Christmas decorations. Your father has to nail the tree in its stand and you two have to decorate it.' For once in her life Mary Moore sounded ratty. Shoving stray strands of hair back into her ponytail, she gave a loud sigh.

3

David Moore came down to ground level to sort everyone out. 'Now listen, let's not panic,' he began. But he didn't see the wet patch on the floor. He skidded and waved his arms, lost his balance and fell down flat. Speckle barked joyfully. Another game! He dashed across and leaped on to the shocked figure, lying full length on the floor.

There was a yell and then silence. Helen looked at Hannah, at the bare tree propped against the wall, the box of decorations next to it. Hannah caught sight of her father's shocked face.

'Speckle, here, boy!' Helen called.

The twins had had the same idea; it was time to make themselves scarce! 'We'll take him for a walk,' Hannah suggested niftily, before their mum and dad had time to object.

Speckle must have heard the word "walk". He bounded straight for the door, leaving Mr Moore sitting bedraggled in a large puddle.

'We'll be back in time to decorate the tree,' Helen called. She'd already escaped out on to the street.

'If you take him to the lake, don't let him go on

the ice. It's not safe!' Mary Moore reminded them.

'Don't worry, we won't!' Hannah grabbed their scarves and gloves from the hat-stand by the door, then made her getaway.

'And don't be too long. We need you here!'

By this time, David Moore had dripped and staggered to the door, still clutching a bunch of mistletoe in one hand. 'No we don't!' he yelled after them. 'Take as long as you like. It's not safe here when you two are around!'

'Charming!' Helen wound her red woollen scarf round her neck and set off with Speckle across the village square towards Nesfield Lake.

'Happy Christmas to you, too!' Hannah muttered, her face twitching into a smile. She glanced at Helen.

Helen giggled. It was a week before Christmas. The sun was shining on a frosty Lake District landscape of high, rocky hills and frozen water. She took in a big lungful of cold clean air and began to sing. ' "On the first day of Christ-mas, my true love sent to me . . . A par-tridge in a pear tree!" '

Speckle howled. Hannah put both hands to her

ears. Together they ran for their lives along the deserted shore.

Half an hour later, Helen was still singing at the top of her voice.

' "On the tenth day of Christmas,
My true love sent to me . . .
Ten lords a-leaping,
Nine maidens dancing,
Eight geese a-laying . . .
Five go-old rings!" '

Hannah threw a stick along the pebbled beach for Speckle and giggled. ' "Fi-ive go-old rings!" ' she echoed.

'So? Why don't you have a go?'

'If I did, I might try and get the words right at least,' Hannah said. 'You've got everything in the wrong order.'

'So?' Helen said again, with a toss of her head. Then she groaned. 'I'm never going to get this right in time for Wednesday.' Wednesday was the last day of term and the day of the Christmas concert. All the mums and dads would be there. 'I'm going to be a laughing-stock!'

'What's that?' Hannah waited for Speckle to come bounding back with the stick. She enjoyed teasing her sister.

'You know!' Suddenly Helen had a glint in her eye. 'Hey, Hannah, I just thought . . . you know how everyone at schools says they can never tell us two apart because we're identical?' She waited for Hannah to catch on. 'And you know how much better you are at singing than me?'

'Uh-oh . . . Oh, no, just hang on a minute!' The penny dropped. Hannah began to shake her head. 'No way am I going to stand up in front of all those people and sing in your place!' It was true, the twins were so alike, they could easily switch around and take each others' places. But Hannah would have died of embarrassment.

'How much?' Helen said quickly. 'A pound?'

'No way!'

'One pound fifty?'

'No.' Hannah flung the stick for Speckle again. The dog chased it then vanished behind a big upturned rowing-boat. 'I wouldn't do it for a thousand pounds.'

'A million?'

'You haven't got a million,' Hannah said scornfully and turned her back.

'Thanks a lot!' Helen scrunched her feet over the pebbles, stamping as she went. She whistled for Speckle to fetch the stick. When he didn't come back, she turned to blame Hannah. 'Now look what you've done. Speckle's run away.'

'I didn't do anything.' Hannah ran on ahead, towards the boat. 'He can't have gone far. Speckle, here, boy!' She whistled for him, expecting him to pop up any minute, carrying the stick clamped between his jaws.

Helen overtook her and jumped on to the boat. 'If he's gone in the water, Mum will kill you,' she muttered. Beneath her feet, under the hollow shell of the wooden hull, she suddenly heard a small scraping and scratching sound.

Hannah heard it too. And she found Speckle sniffing at the boat, whimpering and scrabbling at the pebbles with his front paws. 'What is it, Speckle? What have you found?'

'Something's trapped inside here!' Helen straightaway forgot their quarrel, jumped down and kneeled on the stony ground. She tried to peer under the rim of the boat. 'Hang on a minute, Speckle. Good boy.' From a quick look she saw that the boat had recently tipped from its side into its present position. A length of worn rope had snapped and let it fall. It still swung to and fro, showing them that the accident had only just happened. Now some small creature, who had probably chewed at the rope and made the boat topple, was in there crying to get out.

'Do you think we can lift it?' Hannah tested the weight of the boat.

Helen helped. 'Yep. But we have to be careful. We don't want to frighten whatever is in here even more.'

'OK, I'll wait for you to give the word.' Hannah managed to wriggle her fingers underneath the rim of the boat, ready to lift. The sound from inside had turned from a frantic scratching into a high-pitched whine. The animal must have heard their voices and was cowering in the dark.

Helen got into position. 'Right; one, two, three, lift!'

Their arms took the strain, they heaved. Slowly the boat lifted an inch, then two inches. The whining grew louder as Helen and Hannah jammed big stones in place to prop up the boat. Behind them Speckle sat obediently and whimpered.

At last they raised the boat high enough to peer underneath.

'What is it?' Hannah whispered. It was very dark in there. 'A fox?' She squinted to make her eyes get used to the dim light.

'No, it's too pale for a fox. Over there, see!' Helen spotted the trapped animal. 'I think it's a puppy!'

'Oh, poor thing!' Now Hannah could see it shivering in the far corner; a pale fawn bundle of fur with dark brown, gleaming eyes. 'Come on, Helen, we have to lift the boat a bit higher so we can get him out.'

Once more they heaved at the boat, until there was room for the puppy to creep out. But he stayed put, seemingly terrified. His big eyes glistened, he shivered and shook.

'I don't know how long we can hold this!' Helen whispered. She glanced over her shoulder at Speckle and had an idea. 'Here, boy!' She wanted him to come and help.

Speckle obeyed.

'Tell him it's safe to come out,' Helen gasped. 'Be quick, Speckle, or else we'll have to let the boat drop again.'

The dog seemed to understand the problem. He lowered his head to peer under the boat, saw the puppy and gave a sharp, bossy bark; a kind of, 'Come out of there and stop this nonsense!' bark, as Hannah described it later.

The puppy did as he was told. He saw Speckle's black and white face, heard the order. And, just as the twins' arms began to give way and the boat started to sink back towards the ground, the frightened pup came creeping out from his dark prison into the broad daylight.

Two

Helen and Hannah let the heavy boat drop, then sank to the ground.

'Wow, that was heavy!' Helen groaned.

'I was afraid we were going to squash him as he squeezed his way out.' Hannah admitted that it had been touch and go.

They let Speckle take care of the puppy, getting their breath back and easing their aching shoulders. By the time they'd recovered enough to take in what was happening, the rescued pup had got over his own ordeal and was already firm friends with Speckle.

'Look at that!' Helen grinned. The puppy was bouncing up at the border collie's speckled chest, clinging on to the long fur. He tumbled to the ground and rolled, picked himself up and flung himself at his rescuer once more.

'What a mess!' Hannah laughed. The cream puppy was only a few months old. He was a rough-haired, floppy-eared, dark-eyed, mixture-of-all-sorts mongrel pup. His coat grew in tufts at untidy angles, he was growing a pale moustache and had long grey hairs on his ears. The cream fur on his chest was tangled and knotted, his big paws and little tail were caked with mud. 'You should be called Scruffy!'

'He wants Speckle to play,' Helen laughed. The little puppy was only half the size of their dog, but he was tempting Speckle on to the ice at the edge of the lake. 'No, Speckle!' she warned in a stern voice. 'It's not safe!'

Speckle did as he was told, whining out a warning for the pup to come back.

'I wonder who you belong to.' Hannah went to the water's edge to lift the puppy off the ice. His claws skidded and scratched at the slippery surface, then his legs went from under him. He collapsed into her arms and she scooped him up. 'Come here, you little scamp!'

Helen looked round for his owner. 'He's pretty young to be out all by himself,' she agreed. The beach was still deserted, but she thought she could glimpse a car parked beyond some bushes at the roadside. She pointed it out to Hannah. 'There's your answer,' she guessed. 'You'd think they'd get out of the car to keep an eye on him and stop him getting into mischief, though.'

'Some people are just too lazy.' Hannah hugged

the puppy to her chest. His pink tongue tried to lick her cheek.

'And you'd think they'd be wondering where he'd got to,' Helen went on with a frown.

'Well, it's not anyone we know.' Reluctantly Hannah set the puppy back on his feet. He shook himself down and came and tugged at the bottom of her jeans. The Moores knew practically everyone in the small holiday town of Nesfield, besides all their neighbours on the farms and in the village at Doveton. She stooped to stroke Scruffy's bedraggled coat.

'Maybe it's someone who's just passing through.' Helen saw the driver of the car open the door and get out. Through the bare branches of the bushes she glimpsed a bright red coat. Then they heard a woman's sharp voice calling. 'Oliver, come here at once!'

The puppy pricked up his floppy ears.

'Oliver?' Hannah and Helen said in one breath. They looked down at the untidy scrap of fur playing at their feet.

'. . . That's not a very good name.'

'. . . Scruffy's much better.' They spoke at once.

'Ol-i-ver!' The woman shouted, louder this time.

Scruffy the puppy gave Speckle a longing look and lunged at him one last time. The older dog refused to play. Scruffy's mistress was calling. So the pup gave up and began to trot off up the beach.

'Oliver, come here this minute!' An even louder, even more bad-tempered shout.

The little dog picked up speed.

'Do you think we should go and explain what happened to him?' Hannah asked.

Helen nodded and began to run up the beach. Scruffy had a start on them, but they might be able to reach the road before the car drove off.

But the impatient woman must have been in a big hurry. Her high voice kept on calling the puppy's name, and the second after his shaggy little figure disappeared amongst the bushes, the twins heard a car door slam shut. An engine roared and the gleaming silver car pulled away.

'Too late!' Breathless, Hannah eased off. 'I hope she doesn't tell him off too much.'

'It sounded like she might.' Helen hadn't liked the sound of that harsh voice.

17

There was nothing they could do about it now. Turning to stroke Speckle and tell him what a good boy he'd been, they set off for home.

'Fancy calling him Oliver,' Hannah snorted as they strode along the beach towards the town. She didn't know why, but it just didn't suit the snub-nosed mongrel. A puppy who looked as though he'd been pulled through a hedge backwards needed a name that didn't sound so posh.

'We'll call him Scruffy!' Helen insisted. The Christmas party called them back to the cafe; there was the tree to decorate, mince-pies and sausage-rolls to sample before the guests arrived.

'If we ever see him again.' Hannah sighed. Somehow she didn't believe they would.

By two o'clock that afternoon, everything was baked and decorated, and the party at the Curlew was in full swing.

The tree stood in the corner of the room, coloured lights winking. The tables were piled high with Mary Moore's mince-pies. And the whole room was crowded with all the friends the

Moores had made since they'd arrived in the Lake District.

'He was only about four months old!' Hannah was telling their own friends, Laura Saunders and Sam Lawson about the adventure with the trapped puppy. Her voice rose above the noisy chatter of the other guests. 'He was this big.' She held out her hands to measure Scruffy's size.

'More like this big.' Helen stretched her arms a couple of inches wider apart. 'But he *was* pretty small and really naughty. He kept on wanting to play.' She smiled at the memory of the ragged little puppy.

'I wish I'd seen him,' Laura sighed. Like the twins, she took an interest in all four-legged creatures.

'What for? He was just a mongrel, wasn't he?' Sam pretended not to care. He stuffed another mince-pie into his mouth and went off to talk to his Uncle Luke.

Helen and Hannah made faces at his back. 'Trust Sam!' Helen said.

'Just because he wasn't there when it happened!' Hannah added. Sam's family at Crackpot

Farm were the Moores' nearest neighbours on Doveton Fell, but they didn't always get on with the fair-haired, know-all son. She went on to tell Laura all over again how cute Scruffy had been.

'Never mind that now!' David Moore broke them up. 'No huddling in a corner, girls. It's time to push back the tables and start the disco!'

'Disco! What disco?' This was the first Helen had heard of it. 'Who's the DJ?'

'I am.' Their dad beamed at them. 'And I want to see you all joining in!'

'Da-ad!' Hannah groaned. 'Do we have to?' She looked round the room at the grown-ups in party hats, their faces flushed from drinking too much mulled wine. This was going to be mega-embarrassing.

There was Fred Hunt and John Fox, sturdy old farmers from the Fell, Laura's posh mum and dad from Doveton Manor. Dan and Julie Stott had come over from Clover Farm with baby Joe and they were chatting away to Sophie and Karl Thomas from Rose Terrace just across Nesfield town square. Even Mr Winter, the ex-headteacher at Doveton School was here dressed in his blue blazer with the shiny silver buttons.

'The place is packed with old age pensioners!' Helen hissed in dismay. 'How can we have a disco?'

'Easy!' Mary Moore breezed by. 'Just relax and let your hair down, girls. No one's going to mind if you can't dance very well!'

'Cheek!' Hannah, Helen and Laura chorused.

Mary winked at Val Saunders. 'Let's show these youngsters how it's done,' she said as David Moore began to play the first record.

Before they knew it, the twins and Laura were pushed back into a corner with Sam Lawson by a crowd of weird old people in paper hats, all shaking their hips and flinging their arms in the air.

'Did you see Miss Wesley?' Sam whispered, his mouth open, eyes staring.

Their teacher from Doveton Primary was doing rock and roll with Sam's uncle in the middle of the dance floor. It was Miss Wesley like they'd never seen her before.

'And Mr Winter!' Laura gasped. The normally bad-tempered old man with the drooping moustache held Dotty Miller from Lake View Donkey Sanctuary in his firm grasp. 'They're doing a waltz!'

The sight sent them reeling behind the tree in fits of laughter.

Mary Moore danced past without a partner, spied them giggling and dragged them out again. 'Much more of that and I'll make you sing!' she threatened the twins. She pulled them out on to the floor and forced them to dance.

'Wonderful party!' Laura's father beamed as he jived up to them with his wife. 'The best start to Christmas we've had round here for a long time!'

Laura shook her head as he swayed his shoulders in time to the music. 'How embarrassing!' she muttered between gritted teeth.

'Oh no, you don't!' David Moore had spotted Laura, Sam, Hannah and Helen all trying to slink away towards the door. 'Clear the floor everyone. The next one is especially for the youngsters!' He waited for the floor to empty, then changed the record.

All heads turned to the twins and their friends.

It seemed there was no escape.

Or was there? As Helen went on backing towards the door, she heard the click of the letterbox, saw the flutter of a long, brown envelope as it dropped to the mat. Who could be hand-delivering letters at this time on a Saturday afternoon?

Hannah saw it too and pounced. 'Hang on a minute, this might be important!' She read the address on the back. 'It's for you, Mum. It says it's from Nesfield Council.'

'Oh, never mind, put it down over there on the window-sill and let's have you all dancing!' her dad cried. Nothing was going to spoil his disco session.

But Mary Moore looked puzzled. She took the letter from Hannah and opened it. As she read it, her face fell.

'That was close!' Sam whispered, heaving a sigh of relief.

By now everyone had forgotten about them dancing and had turned to look at Mary Moore. They waited for her to finish reading.

David Moore turned down the volume. The

chatter and the laughter died away. 'What is it, Mary?'

'They can't do this, surely!' Her voice was strained when she spoke. 'Not without asking us first.'

'Can't do what?' Barbara Wesley came forward to see if she could help.

The twins watched as their mother held out the letter with a shaking hand. 'Well, if I understand what they're telling me here, they say they're going to close the square to all traffic!'

'When?'

'Why?'

'For how long?'

She was bombarded with questions, but Mary Moore shook her head and ignored them. 'No cars?' she said, trying to make sense of what she'd been told.

'Surely not!'

'They can't do that!'

No one believed that the local council could possibly mean it.

David Moore joined his wife and took the letter from her. 'They say it's for redevelopment of the square,' he explained. 'They have big plans to bring more tourists in next summer.'

Now serious faces crowded round to see what it meant.

'No cars?' the twins' mum repeated, more faintly than before. 'That means no customers!'

She looked round helplessly at all their friends gathered together for the Christmas party. 'What they're really telling me is that the Curlew Cafe will have to close!'

Three

'What does it mean exactly?' Helen asked her dad the next day.

It was early Sunday morning and they were out in the barn at Home Farm. Hannah stuffed fresh hay into Solo's manger and brought clean water for him to drink. The grey pony waited patiently while she filled his bucket.

'What does what mean?' The twins' normally cheerful dad asked. He looked serious, leaning against the doorpost, watching them work.

'Redevelopment.' Helen stumbled over the long word.

David Moore sighed. 'It means that workmen are going to come and dig the square up in the New Year.'

'What for?' Hannah patted Solo's neck and smiled up at him. He snickered and nuzzled her hand.

'The council thinks the place needs improving. It's like a face-lift, only on a big scale. New pavements, new seats for people to sit on, a new market area for the stall holders.'

'Isn't it OK as it is?' Helen liked the look of the old place, with its stone cobbles and higgledy-piggledy appearance.

'Most of us who live round here happen to think so,' Mr Moore murmured. There had nearly been a riot when Mary had announced the news at the party. Neighbours from the square had received their own letters and come rushing into the Curlew, demanding to know what was going on. There was the man from the fishing-tackle shop across the square, the woman who ran the post-office next door. They were both shaking their heads and saying they couldn't believe it, and what on earth were they going to do?

'Can't you go and tell the council to leave the square alone?' Hannah asked her dad. She only had a vague idea of what a town council was. To her it was just a room full of people in a grand building who made arrangements to have your dustbin emptied and your streets cleaned.

'If only!' Their dad explained that it was a lot more complicated than that. He insisted that he liked the quaint old square just as it was. 'Once these people have decided to "improve" something, there's no stopping them.'

'But Mum says that if they close the square while they're working on it, she won't get any customers in the cafe.' The council thing might be hard to understand, but it didn't seem difficult to see what this would mean to the Curlew. 'How long will they take?'

'That's one of the problems; a couple of months at least. The road through town will have to be closed off. Your mother can't afford to lose her customers for that long.'

The twins nodded. They knew that their mum didn't make much money from the cafe as it was. But she loved working there, meeting people and selling them her wonderful cakes and biscuits. And she was good at it too.

'It makes me really mad!' Helen frowned as she swept the barn floor clear of Solo's old straw.

'Mum's upset, isn't she?' Hannah asked quietly.

Their dad nodded. 'She loves that cafe. It means the world to her.' Then he gave a shrug and turned towards the house. 'Well, I'd better drive into town and try to cheer her up a bit.' Mary Moore worked on a Sunday, then had Monday off. 'Do you two fancy coming?'

He needn't have asked. Helen and Hannah finished their jobs and hopped into the car with Speckle before their dad had changed his shoes. They drove out of the farmyard and down the lane deep in thought.

'You're quiet back there,' David Moore said as they passed along the main street in tiny Doveton village. Luke Martin gave them a wave from the doorway of his shop, Mr Winter marched briskly along the pavement with his Cairn terrier, Puppy. It was a clear morning with a nip in the air; still too early for many people to be about.

'We're thinking!' Hannah told him.

They drove on in silence, along the winding pass between the sheer fells towards Nesfield. The hills were covered in thick white frost, the jagged horizon standing out against a pale blue sky.

'Well, don't overdo it,' he joked, unnerved by the silence from the back seat. They were coming down the hill into Nesfield, with a view of the greeny-blue slate roofs. Thin wisps of smoke curled from the chimneys. Then they were in the town, winding through the narrow streets until they came to the market square in the centre.

There was Rose Terrace and there was the Curlew, with its bright checked curtains and lights shining out a warm welcome on this cold day.

David Moore stopped nearby to let the twins and Speckle hop out. 'I'll park properly and follow you,' he promised. 'And remember, don't be a nuisance. Your mum has enough on her plate!'

A nuisance? Hannah looked as if butter wouldn't melt. She swung into the cafe. 'Hi, Mum!' She unzipped her jacket and flung it over a chair. 'Have you got any paper?'

'Yes. What for?' In between serving customers, Mary Moore took some clean sheets from a drawer behind the counter. She looked weary; not her usual bright self.

'And a felt-tip pen?' Hannah asked.

'I've got one.' Helen dug into her pocket. 'What do we need them for?'

'Wait and see.' Hannah sat at a table and got to work with pen and paper. Helen peered over her shoulder as she began to write.

' "Save Our Square!" ' David Moore read. He took the piece of paper from the table and read the slogan.

' "Hands Off Nesfield!" ' Mary Moore read another carefully written message. She looked thoughtfully at the twins. 'Whose idea was this?'

'Hannah's,' Helen told them. 'How about it?' She hopped excitedly from one foot to the other. 'I think it's brilliant, don't you?'

'It's a petition,' Hannah explained. 'We've got to get everyone to sign it and send it to the council.' She looked up at her mum and dad with shining eyes. 'If enough people say they want them to leave the square alone, they'll have to listen!'

'Hmm.' Mrs Moore thought it through. A couple of customers had wandered across to find out what was going on.

David Moore gave them the 'Save Our Square' notice to read. 'It might already be too late,' he warned the twins. 'Work's due to start on January the second; that's only two weeks away.' He explained the problem to the sympathetic customers.

'But we can try!' Hannah insisted.

'It's better than doing nothing,' Helen agreed.

'Give me a pen. I'll sign it!' one of the customers

offered. He was an elderly man wrapped up in a scarf and woolly hat, wearing sturdy walking-boots. 'I've been coming here for over thirty years,' he told them. 'I think the old market square is grand just as it is.' He wrote his name with a flourish.

'Our first signature!' Hannah seized the paper from the table. 'See!'

'It's only one name, remember.' Mrs Moore didn't want to get her hopes up.

'Two!' The old man's wife offered to add her name to the list.

Soon another group of customers had been drawn in. Now there were seven names asking the council to save the square.

'Let's pin the petition up in the window,' Hannah suggested, thrilled by her success so far.

'Go on, Mum!' Helen didn't see what they had to lose. 'We've got a whole week before Christmas, and a whole week after. We can get thousands of signatures by then!'

Still she hesitated, gazing down at the empty 'Hands Off Nesfield!' sheet. 'What do you think,

David?' she asked. 'Do you suppose people will care enough to sign up?'

Helen and Hannah nodded, itching for him to say yes. But they knew not to push any harder. It had been Hannah's idea, but their mum and dad were the ones to decide.

David Moore smiled and put his arm around his wife's shoulder. 'When people realise what this means; that there'll be no more homemade cakes and hot chocolate waiting for them after a tiring day on Doveton Fell, you bet they'll care!' he told her. 'In fact, we need another notice,' he told the twins.

Helen grabbed a fresh sheet of paper and a pen. 'What do you want me to write this time?'

'Nice big letters, so people can read it in the window,' he instructed. Slowly he spelled out the message. ' "Support The Curlew! Say No to Council Improvements!" ' Then he turned to hug the twins' mum.

'We can't let the best cafe in the whole of the Lake District close down without a fight,' he said.

Four

By Sunday evening, the Moores' 'Save The Curlew' petition had collected fifty-three signatures. On Monday, Christmas shoppers in Nesfield had added another eighty-five names. By the end of Tuesday, the total was two hundred and twelve, and a man from the council had telephoned the cafe to find out what it was all about.

Helen and Hannah were helping Mary Moore out after school.

'Mu-um, it's for you!' Helen called. Her mind was on other things as she handed over the phone.

'What's up with you?' Hannah was busy

counting signatures, planning to take the petition into school next day for the teachers to sign.

' "On the seventh day of Christ-mas my true love sent to me . . ." ' Helen muttered under her breath. ' "On the seventh day of Christ-mas . . . !" ' She was stuck again. Tomorrow was Wednesday; the day of the school concert.

Hannah grinned and glanced up. She saw a knot of people reading one of the notices in the window and rushed out into the street to get them to sign.

'That's four more!' she told Helen as the fell walkers added their names and went on their way. Her sister had followed her outside with Speckle. 'You could look a bit more pleased about it.'

Helen was frowning and peering across the square. 'Four names? That's great.'

'And you could sound as if you mean it too!' Hannah was cross. 'What's so interesting?'

'I'm not sure.' Helen took a couple of steps across the pavement. 'Hannah, you see that car parked over there?'

'The silver one?' She could see it all right, but what was special? To Hannah it looked like any other car.

'Don't you recognise it?'

'Nope.' It was too cold to hang about outside so she turned to head back inside.

'Isn't it the one we saw by the lake?' Once an idea grabbed Helen, she hung on tight. 'You know; last Saturday.'

Hannah paused. 'Scruffy's car?'

Speckle seemed to prick up his ears, looking from one twin to the other.

'Yes.' Helen was halfway across the square. If she was right, she didn't want to miss the chance to see their sweet little friend.

'I don't think so, Helen.' Doubtfully Hannah tagged along, calling Speckle to come too. But then she saw a flash of red, a tall slim figure with fair hair disappearing down a side street, high heels clicking, head held high. Hadn't the woman by the lake been wearing a red coat? Hannah broke into a run to catch up with her sister.

'What did I tell you?' Helen hissed. The big silver car stood outside Mr Bassett's fishing-tackle shop, half blocking a side street. She pointed to a dog grille fixed across the back of the estate car and the back window smeared with muddy paws.

'Scruffy!' It was more than Hannah had dared to hope. To see the messy pup again; to discover that he lived nearby would be a dream come true. She pictured more lakeside walks, more fun and games. 'Speckle, do you know whose car this is?' she asked, bending down to talk to him. 'Is Scruffy in there?'

'I don't think so.' Helen peered inside. There was a torn checked blanket, a chewed rubber ball. But no puppy.

Disappointed, Hannah looked down the street.

'Oliver!' A woman's voice called. They could hear her but not see her.

Helen and Hannah stared at each other. Their hunch had been right.

'Oliver, come here!' the woman commanded. 'You're a naughty little dog! If you don't come here this minute, I'll give you such a smack!'

They got set to follow her down the narrow street.

'Speckle will find him for her,' Hannah suggested. 'We can bring the puppy back and tell her who we are. She might even let us take him for walks . . . !'

'Hold on, we've got to find him first.' Helen listened to the sound of the woman's heels clicking along the pavement.

'Which way, Speckle?' Hannah knew they could trust their border collie to track Scruffy down.

But before he had time to pick up the trail, there was a shout from across the square.

'*Helen-Hannah*, come here quick!'

It was their mum calling, running their names into one, meaning that it was urgent.

She spotted them and waved. 'Quickly!' she called again. 'I've got some news!'

So, reluctantly, they gave up their plan and sped back to the cafe. Meeting up with Scruffy's owner would have to wait until another time.

'What?' Hannah arrived first, dashing through the door, out of the cold into the cosy warmth.

'Good news or bad?' Helen demanded.

Mary Moore was pacing up and down, wiping her hands on her striped apron. 'Good, I think.'

'From the council man?'

'Yes, Mr Bottomley. He works for a Miss O'Connor. She's the one who makes all the big decisions.'

'About the work on the square?' Hannah could tell that this was important. Her mum's face was flushed red with excitement, she could hardly keep still.

She nodded. 'He says they've heard about our petition. Someone from the local newspaper rang the council office to ask questions. Mr Bottomley told Miss O'Connor about it and she's agreed to have a meeting with us!'

'That's great!' Hannah sank back into a chair. 'We've made them listen!'

'Yes, but we haven't won the argument yet.' Mary Moore forced herself to calm down. 'One thing at a time. Mr Bottomley says that he and Miss O'Connor will come here on Friday to talk to us.'

'That's Christmas Eve. We'll have hundreds more names by then!' Helen's hopes rose.

'He says Miss O'Connor came to town today to have another look at the problem. It does sound as if they're taking us seriously.' Their mum sighed.

'On the other hand, they could just be pre-tending to listen to us, so that we keep quiet.

You never know with these people.' She grew more uneasy. 'Oh, girls, I'm in such a muddle I don't know what to think!'

'What are you getting so upset about?' Hannah wanted to know, first thing next morning. It was as if the whole house was on edge.

Helen had told off Socks, their little tabby cat, for putting dirty paw prints all over the latest sheet of the petition. She'd pushed him away and now he was hiding under the kitchen table, wondering what he'd done wrong.

'Nothing!' Helen insisted she wasn't upset.

'Yes, you are.'

'Stop arguing, you two.' Mary Moore swept through the kitchen on her way to work. 'Be good. I'll see you at school this afternoon.' She'd promised to come to the Christmas concert to hear Helen sing.

'You don't have to come if you're too busy.' Helen gave it one last try. If there was one thing she dreaded, it was making a fool of herself. She cleaned up the paper that Socks had trodden on and put it carefully into her school bag.

'Nonsense, love. I wouldn't miss it for the world.' Mary winked at Hannah.

'Neither would I,' David Moore agreed. He planned to take an afternoon off from his work developing photographs in the attic darkroom. 'A chance for us to see our little girl on stage! We're going to be so proud!'

'Huh!' Helen slung her bag over her shoulder and stomped off to the car.

A few minutes later Hannah joined her, humming 'The Twelve Days of Christmas' under her breath. 'Last day of school before the holidays!' she sighed, easing herself into the back seat. 'I can't wait.'

'Hannah . . .' Helen began in a wheedling, whining voice.

'Nope!' Hannah cut her short.

'Five pounds?' she pleaded. Surely Hannah wouldn't mind making a fool of herself for five whole pounds. The song came right at the end of the concert, before school broke up for two weeks.

'No way!'

'Ready?' Mary Moore got into the car. She

would drop them off at school in Doveton, then drive on to Nesfield to work. 'Remember to let Barbara Wesley sign the petition,' she reminded them.

'I don't know how Miss Wesley can be so cruel,' Helen moaned.

' "On the first day of Christ-mas . . ." ' Hannah sang.

Mrs Moore ignored them. 'And any of the other teachers who want to support us. The more signatures we have by Friday the better.'

'I can't even remember the words!' Helen wailed. 'What am I going to do?'

'It'll be all right on the night,' her mum said, setting them down by the school gate. 'Honestly, Helen, don't worry. No one will mind if you go a little bit wrong.'

'I will.' She got out of the car, hanging her head. 'I don't feel very well, Mum. I've got a bit of a sore throat.'

Mary Moore looked at her and laughed. 'Nice try, Helen!'

There was no way out of it.

' "Ten lords a-leaping, Nine geese a-laying . . ." '

Hannah mangled the words as they crossed the frozen playground.

Helen bashed her with her schoolbag, then they disappeared into the cloakroom to start the dreaded day.

For Hannah the hours of the last day of school dragged by. She couldn't wait for the Christmas holiday to start.

But for Helen the morning went in a flash. Then it was afternoon; time for the concert.

'Line up at the door, please!' Miss Wesley clapped her hands after she finished calling the register. 'Now, Class 6, I want you to listen carefully!' She warned them to be on their best behaviour. 'We have some important visitors in school this afternoon. Many of your parents are coming to join us for our concert, and I know you will want to put on a good show for them.'

Helen felt her mouth go dry and the palms of her hands grow sticky. She hung back at the end of the queue. ' "On the fifth day of Christ-mas . . ." ' she muttered under her breath, then she got stuck. She couldn't even remember ' "Five go-old rings!" '

Miss Wesley went on. 'And we also have some new school governors coming to join us, so we'll really want to impress!' When she was sure that everyone understood, she ordered the line to move off towards the assembly hall. 'Come along, Helen,' she urged, waiting to close the classroom door behind her. 'We haven't got all day!'

Helen's feet felt like lead, her legs seemed to have turned to jelly.

'Catch up with Hannah, there's a good girl. It's not like you to be so slow!' Cheerily the teacher herded them along the corridor.

'Here come Mum and Dad!' Hannah glanced out of a window to see them crossing the play-ground amongst a crowd of other parents. She smiled and waved.

Helen kept her head down, dragging one foot after another. 'Nightmare!' she muttered, wiping her sweaty palms on her skirt.

She was so nervous as she took her place on the stage that she couldn't take in a single thing. There was a sea of faces staring up at her, a glare of spotlights. In the front seats she glimpsed a row of well-dressed visitors, all sitting up straight, politely waiting.

Then Miss Wesley played the first notes on the piano. The terrible moment had come.

Year 3 sang their Christmas carols, the Reception class acted out the story of Jesus's birth. Eve Lawson, Sam's youngest sister, was Mary. She forgot to bring the baby Jesus doll on stage, so the shepherds and the wise men had to worship an empty crib.

'How sweet!' the audience murmured.

'Look at the angels! Aren't they lovely?'

'Now they were in full swing. The nativity play drew to a close, the audience clapped, and the time for Helen's solo crept nearer.

'OK?' Hannah leaned sideways to whisper. Helen's face had gone a ghastly white.

'No!' she gasped through dry lips.

'It's your turn!' Hannah jogged her in the side with her elbow. 'Go on, Helen!'

Her head swam as she stood up and moved to the front of the stage. She wished the lights would melt her or that the ground would swallow her up. Down in the hall, all eyes were on her. Miss Wesley played her introduction. Helen opened her mouth, ready to begin.

But there was a murmur spreading through the audience, rising like a wave to a gasp and then a cry. The children nearest the door began to giggle.

' "On the first day of Christ-mas . . ." ' Helen boldly tried to ignore the interruption.

'Wait!' Miss Wesley stopped playing and got up from the piano.

Helen's voice trailed off, her mouth hung open. She turned to Hannah.

'Look!' Hannah jumped up from her seat and pointed from the stage down into the crowded hall. Through all the confusion she could just see what was happening.

The door had been left open to let in some fresh air and now they had an unexpected visitor. A floppy-eared, panting, cream-coloured intruder.

'Where did he come from?' someone cried.

'Aah!' the children gasped in delight at the sight of the yapping puppy.

'Stop him!' Miss Wesley pleaded.

It was Scruffy! Hannah would have known him

anywhere. He wound in and out of the chairs, snuffling and sniffing. He must have been left in a car in the car park and escaped. Now he was causing chaos in the concert hall.

'Thank heavens!' Helen sighed. Chairs scraped, people stood up and milled about. No one gave another thought to her closing song. All they wanted to know was who the puppy belonged to!

'You jammy thing!' Hannah came up to Helen and grinned. Luck was on Helen's side; Miss Wesley had given up and waved them all down from the stage. It was time to go home.

Helen beamed from ear to ear. She spied the unstoppable pup sneaking between a forest of legs and back out of the door the way he'd come.

'Thank you, Scruffy!' she sighed. 'You saved my life!'

Five

'How come you know this dog?' David Moore quizzed the twins as they drove home from school. Light snow was falling, sprinkling the hills with pretty flakes that glittered in the car head-lights.

'We don't know him exactly,' Hannah explained.

'But we wish we did.' Helen pondered the mystery of who Scruffy could belong to. There'd been such chaos in the assembly hall as school broke up for the holiday that they'd had no chance to find out.

'Funnily enough, I've seen him round and about

the square these last few days,' Mary Moore told them. She was sitting in the front seat, sifting through the lists of new signatures they'd got for their petition. 'He always seems to be getting into mischief somehow. Peter Bassett was telling me he had to drag him out of his window display of fishing-rods and nets yesterday. The little scamp had got himself seriously tangled up. And the other funny thing is, there never seems to be an owner in charge of him!'

'We know!' Hannah sighed. 'We've been hoping to meet her.'

'Her?' Mary raised her eyebrows. 'How do you even know that much?'

They explained about the blonde figure in the red coat, the high voice calling for Oliver.

'Oliver!' David Moore snorted. 'He didn't look much like an Oliver to me!'

'I know. He's too friendly and floppy to be an Oliver,' Helen agreed.

'And his coat always needs a brush,' Hannah added.

'And he needs some proper training.'

'Like Speckle.'

'*We* could do it!' Helen sighed, gazing out of the window at the floating snowflakes.

'But you don't know the first thing about him. I'd forget it if I were you,' their dad advised.

'We can't,' Helen and Hannah said in the same breath, their dark eyes shining. 'How can we ignore him when we're so worried about him?'

School was over and Helen and Hannah plunged into the two day rush up to Christmas. Thursday: presents to buy for their mum and dad, last minute cards to send. They hung paper chains from the ceilings at Home Farm and made silver decorations out of pine cones and holly. A stack of brightly wrapped parcels grew steadily under the tree in the front room.

Friday: Christmas Eve. Luckily for everyone, the snow that had fallen on the Wednesday hadn't amounted to much. It had left a thin, crisp covering that had frozen hard on the hillsides and icy lakes. 'Like a scene on a Christmas card,' David Moore said as he drove the twins and Speckle into town for the Big Meeting.

'Who'll be there?' Hannah asked. The meeting

with the council officials was due to take place at the Curlew in an hour's time, at three o'clock. They'd promised their mum that they would arrive early and help her get ready.

'Everyone.'

'Like who?' Hannah insisted. There wasn't room in the cafe for everyone who'd signed their petition. At the last count, they had nearly six hundred names on the list.

'Like, Peter Bassett and the other shopkeepers on the square. Sophie and Karl Thomas have promised to be there to put the residents' point of view. Barbara Wesley wants to have her say, and Luke Martin, and Mr and Mrs Saunders, and Mr Winter . . .' He reeled off the names as they drove into the square. 'Oh, and Mr Bottomley and Miss O'Connor from the council, of course.'

'And Mum wants us to serve them all with coffee and mince-pies,' Helen reminded them. It sounded like they were going to be busy. She ordered Speckle out of the car, ready to begin.

But their dad held them back. 'Hang on, girls, while I get my camera.' He reached into the glove-compartment. 'I want to take some pictures of you and Speckle in the square before the council workmen get their hands on it and ruin the place.' Photography was his job, so the pictures were bound to come out well. 'We might even be able to use them in our fight to stop them making these so-called improvements!'

So he lined them up against the stone columns of the market hall, sat them on the broad steps around the war memorial, had them standing by the Christmas tree that stood proudly in the middle of the cobbled square. 'Great!' he kept saying as he clicked away.

Helen and Hannah's faces grew stiff with smiling. Speckle behaved perfectly, posing for the camera with his ears pricked, his head held high. At last Mr Moore was through and he let them go inside. He went off to the chemists to get the photos developed on the spot. 'Tell your mum what I'm up to!' he called as they nipped inside.

'Yuck!' Helen hated having her picture taken. She was about to take off her jacket and scarf when their mum came rushing out of the kitchen and spotted them.

'Oh good, there you are! Just in time. We need

six more tubs of double cream from the little supermarket on the edge of town. You know the one?'

Helen and Hannah nodded.

'Six tubs of cream and six cartons of pasteurised milk. Do you think you can manage to carry them?' Mary rushed from table to table with pretty silver decorations. She wanted to put on a good show for the people from the council.

'No problem.' Hannah took some money and told Speckle to come with them.

'Be as quick as you can.'

The twins zipped up and hurried out with Speckle. 'Six tubs of double cream,' Helen repeated under her breath, in case they forgot.

' "Six tubs of cre-eam, nine lords a-leaping, eight maids a-milking . . . five go-old rings!" ' Hannah laughed, making the tune fit.

'Huh!' Helen ran ahead. As a matter of fact, she could remember the words to the song perfectly now that she didn't need to. She stuck her nose in the air and went into the shop for the cream and milk, giving the six cartons to Hannah to carry and keeping the cream for herself.

'Do you need a bag?' the girl at the till asked.

'No thanks.' Hannah was in a hurry to get back.

And they set off, through the narrow streets, past Bassett's shop, back into the square, juggling the cartons unsteadily as they ran.

'Watch out, it's slippy!' Helen jumped over a puddle by the kerb. It was covered in thick ice.

Hannah swerved and missed it by inches. The stack of milk cartons wobbled. 'Wait!' she warned. Steadying them, they heard a car draw up in a parking-space nearby. It meant they had to move along the pavement for a better view before they crossed the square.

'Here, Speckle, good boy!' Helen made him wait with them.

But the car door had opened and a woman was scolding someone or something inside the car. 'Stay!' she ordered in a high, strained voice.

In the same split second Hannah and Helen recognised that voice. They knew the wild, yapping bark and the hairy cream shape that came flying out of the door towards them.

They didn't even have time to take a step back

before the puppy launched himself at Speckle, overjoyed to see his friend.

'Oliver, come here!' This time the woman had really lost her temper. She came storming after him.

Of course, he ignored her. He rolled on the ground, picked himself up, threw himself at Helen, who stepped onto the icy puddle, slipped and fell. Her legs shot from under her, slicing against Hannah's feet. Hannah lost her balance, flung out her arms and landed alongside her sister. The tubs of cream and cartons of milk went up in the air and fell to the ground in big white splodges.

'Oliver, stop!' The woman was beside herself with anger. But she was helpless. She watched her puppy dance with delight in the middle of the mess he'd made, licking at the cream with his pink tongue, rolling in the puddle of milk.

'Woah!' David Moore came running up clutching his packet of photographs. He lunged for Scruffy and missed.

'Oliver, look what you've done!' the woman wailed. The cold wind was ruffling her neat blonde hair, her shiny black high-heeled shoes

were spattered with cream. 'I'm terribly sorry!' she told the twins' dad. 'I can't get him to listen to a word I say!'

'That's OK.' Mr Moore held out a hand to haul Hannah to her feet. 'No use crying over spilled milk, eh?' He made a feeble joke of it.

Helen groaned and stood up. But the sight of Scruffy lapping up the cream, covered in the stuff, made her smile in spite of everything. There he was, gobbling to his heart's content, ignoring the chaos he'd caused.

'Try and grab him,' her dad told her. 'Take him by surprise while he's not looking.'

So she crept up from behind. The puppy was so busy snuffling and lapping at the mess that he didn't notice her. Quickly she snatched him. He yelped and wriggled, but he was trapped.

'Well done.' David Moore tried to give the dog a wipe down with his handkerchief. Scruffy shook his head and wriggled some more. Helen held tight.

'No, give him to me,' the woman ordered.

Helen glanced at her dad, who nodded. So she handed Scruffy over to his angry owner.

'You naughty, naughty little dog!' The woman seized him and gave him a sharp slap.

Scruffy yelped.

Hannah grimaced at Helen. There was no need to hit him so hard.

'Silly, silly boy!' With each word she gave him another heavy smack.

Scruffy wriggled and howled.

Ouch! Helen felt her eyes begin to smart. Hannah couldn't bear to look.

'Now-let-that-be-a-lesson-to-you!' Eight more smacks on the poor puppy's nose. Then the woman shook him hard.

'Don't do that!' Hannah said under her breath. She turned away.

Leave him alone! Hannah wanted to shout it out loud, to stop the woman from being so cruel.

'It's OK, really!' Mr Moore tried to step in.

'You disgusting, messy, disobedient little creature!' Still she shook him as she carried him off to the car. 'I can't take you anywhere without you running off and doing something dreadful!' Roughly she threw him down in the back of the car and slammed the door.

Then she took a deep breath, came back to David Moore and offered to pay for the spoiled cartons.

The twins' dad took the money quietly. From inside the car they could hear Scruffy's painful cries.

'And I really am most awfully sorry,' the woman said, back in control of her temper at last. She tried to give a smile, but it came out stiff and false. 'I must admit that Oliver has caused me a lot of problems since I came to live in Nesfield. It almost makes me wish I could take him back to the dogs' home where I found him!'

Six

'Maybe she was just being firm.' Mary Moore hurried about the room. As she set out cups and saucers, plates, and serviettes, she listened to Helen and Hannah's nightmare story about the smart woman and her puppy. There was only a quarter of an hour left before people began to arrive for the meeting.

'No, Mum. She was hitting him so hard I thought he was going to break!' Hannah winced at the memory.

'And shaking him,' Helen added. 'She said she wanted to send him back to the dogs' home!'

65

'He was only doing what all puppies do!' Hannah took jugs of cream from the counter to the tables. Their dad had slipped back to the shop to buy more after they'd cleaned up the accident in the square. 'He wants to play, that's all.'

'But an owner has to show a dog who's boss.' Mary believed in firmness. She'd lived in the country herself when she was a child, and knew that the easiest way to ruin an animal was to spoil him. 'Once you've gained his respect, that's when you can begin to make a fuss of him.'

'What do you mean?' Helen stopped to think. She was standing at the door, looking out, waiting for people to arrive.

'Well, think about Speckle, for instance.'

Their dog pricked up his ears. His tail wagged gently from side to side.

'He was a stray when you found him. We don't know where he came from, and he certainly hadn't had anyone spending time with him, training him to do as he was told.'

The twins remembered their climb down into the dangerous, disused quarry to rescue Speckle when he was a puppy.

'And you remember how you were with him, teaching him to sit by praising him when he got it right?'

They nodded. Speckle had been a lively, mischievous pup, just like Scruffy.

'And how you used to have to push him down when you said the word "Sit!", and pushing him down again if he stood up, until he stayed down and understood?'

Again they nodded.

'Well, that's what I mean by being firm.'

'But we never smacked him!' Hannah protested. She couldn't get the sound of Scruffy's cries out of her head. By now she'd begun to see his harsh owner as a kind of witch; long red fingernails, sharp nose poking out of her face, red lips, a cruel smile.

'That's true.' Mary Moore stood still for a second and smiled kindly at her two girls. 'I'm sorry you're upset, but listen, we'll talk about it later. Right now we have to concentrate on persuading the people from the council not to close down the square.'

'Ready for the coffee-pots?' David Moore called

from the kitchen. He appeared at the door with two steaming metal pots.

'Yep. Here come the first people!' Helen spotted Peter Bassett and his wife crossing the square.

'OK, run and fetch the mince pies!' Mary told Hannah, sweeping back into action.

And soon the cafe bell was ringing to the sound of more people crowding in for the meeting; Karl Thomas from Rose Terrace, Pauline, the ex-post-office mistress, the Moores' friends from Doveton, all complaining about the cold and panicking because they were nowhere near ready for Christmas.

'So where's this Mr Bottomley chap and Miss What'sername?' Old Fred Hunt from High Hartwell looked at his watch. 'I haven't got all day.'

'Miss O'Connor. They said they'd be here by three.' Mary Moore grew anxious. 'What if they've changed their minds?' It would mean that the council would just go ahead with the work on January the second and the petition would all have been a waste of time.'

The old farmer sniffed. 'Don't you worry,' he told her. 'If they don't turn up, we'll go straight out of here and march on the Town Hall, the whole gang of us! That'll soon make them sit up and take notice.'

For Fred Hunt this was a long speech. Helen and Hannah nodded eagerly, ready to head the march. No way were they going to give up now.

'No need for that.' Karl Thomas had stationed himself by the window. 'Here come a man and a woman I've never seen before!'

As soon as he made his announcement, the whole room fell quiet. Everyone stopped chatting or drinking coffee and held their breath.

'How do they look?' Helen wanted to know. She tried to squeeze through the packed crowd so that she could see the two council people arrive. But her way was blocked.

'Serious or cheerful?' Hannah asked. She waited to hear the ring of the doorbell as the door swung open.

'Serious,' Karl reported back to them. 'Especially the woman. The man doesn't look so bad.'

'Stand back.' Fred Hunt ordered people to make a space so that the council officials could squeeze in. 'Let the dog see the rabbit!'

'What rabbit? What dog?' Hannah whispered to Helen. She felt herself pushed further back, behind the counter.

'There's no rabbit, silly!' Helen decided to stand on a stool to see. 'He means give them room to get in!' She peered over the heads of the grown-ups. 'Here they come now!'

The doorbell jangled, Hannah stood on a second stool. The man came in first. He had black hair slicked back from his face, a smart collar and tie. Then she saw the woman and her mouth fell open.

'What? What?' Helen jostled to see.

Hannah pointed at the woman's neatly combed, smooth blonde hair, her red lipstick. She saw the tilt of her head as she came in, a patterned silk scarf around her neck, a bright red coat.

And now Helen could see her too. 'You mean . . . that's Miss O'Connor?' She closed her mouth and swallowed hard.

The twins' mum went forward to meet the

visitors. 'Hello. Welcome to the Curlew Cafe.' She showed them in, offered them a cup of coffee and a place at one of the tables.

'But that's . . . !' Hannah still couldn't believe it. But there was no mistaking the pointed nose, the painted fingernails. 'That's Scruffy's owner!' she gasped.

Now the twins had a double reason to hate her.

'She hits her puppy!' Helen whispered darkly to Fred Hunt.

The farmer tutted and frowned.

'She wants to close down our cafe!' Hannah hissed to anyone who could hear.

'You can tell she's cruel.' Helen studied her thin face and high forehead. Sitting at the table opposite their lovely, kind mum, Miss O'Connor looked proud and cool.

'She doesn't look as if she's listening to a word Mum says!' Hannah cried. But the meeting had at least got underway.

'Shh!' someone in the crowd warned. 'I'm trying to listen!'

'. . . And we have considered this plan to

improve the square in great detail,' Miss O'Connor was saying in that high, grating voice. 'What Nesfield needs is a fresh image; nice new benches and litter-bins made to look old-fashioned and in keeping with the style of the houses. And the plan is to keep the old stone cobbles, but to lift them one by one and lay them down flat for a smoother surface.'

'Pah!' Fred Hunt couldn't resist a scornful pop of his lips.

Miss O'Connor ignored the interruption. 'Of course, the work will cost the council a lot of money, but we think it will be worth it in the long run.'

Mr Bottomley nodded his head in agreement.

'But what will happen to our shops and cafes in the meantime?' Mary Moore wanted to know. 'If you block the square off so that no one can get near, we won't have any customers. We'll all have to close, and you'll end up with nice new litter-bins and benches, but rows of empty shops!'

'Hear-hear!' a few people cried.

Miss O'Connor waved her slender hand, pushing away their objections. 'Surely you can close

down for a couple of weeks, take a holiday, which I'm sure you all deserve, and then open up again when the work's finished!'

This time Mr Bottomley ducked his head, embarrassed. A few more people went 'Pah!'

'We've got a petition,' Mary Moore went on. 'There are nearly six hundred names all saying that we like the square the way it is.' She pushed a pile of signed sheets across the table.

Miss O'Connor took it with a sigh. 'We'll read it, of course . . .'

'But?' Mary Moore wanted to put the council

official on the spot. 'What are you saying? That you'll read it but you won't take any notice of it?'

'I wouldn't say that.' The woman cleared her throat, picked up her shiny black handbag and got ready to leave.

'What would you say?' Mary Moore was frowning, standing up too. Chairs scraped, people shuffled out of the way, disappointed.

'That we'll read your petition, Mrs Moore.' There was a snap of her bag as the papers were shoved inside. 'And we'll let you know our decision as soon as possible.'

She turned, her heels clicked over the tiled floor. Mr Bottomley, his head still hanging, trailed after his boss. Once more the doorbell jangled and they were gone.

Seven

The short day drew to a close. Street lights came on in Nesfield square as Mary Moore's friends and supporters quietly left the cafe.

'Keep your chin up,' Fred Hunt told her. 'We haven't lost the battle yet.' He pulled his cap low over his forehead and stepped out into the frosty evening.

'He's right.' David Moore slipped his arm around Mary's waist. 'At least Miss O'Connor sat and listened to your side of the story.'

Hannah agreed, trying to look on the bright side. 'And Mr Bottomley was nowhere near as

75

horrible as Miss O'Connor.'

But Helen stood in the doorway, looking out at the Christmas tree lights twinkling in the dusk. Her heart was sinking into her boots as she thought of the woman's sharp, pinched expression and she remembered how cruel she'd been to poor little Scruffy.

Her mum came up behind her. 'How could they even think about "improving" this place?' she sighed.

The coloured lights winked, the frost glistened on the stone cobbles, and all the shop windows around the square glowed warm yellow.

Christmas Eve. Almost time to close the cafe and go home.

'It's going to be a strange sort of Christmas,' Mary confessed, ready to pull down the blind. 'Not knowing how long we'll be able to stay open in the New Year.'

Helen put a hand on her arm. 'Wait a minute, Mum!' She'd spotted Miss O'Connor hurrying back across the square. 'What does she want now?'

She was by herself, her coat flew open in the

cold wind, she was breaking into a run.

'Maybe she forgot her umbrella or something.' Hannah took a quick look under the table where the woman from the council had been sitting.

Yes, Miss O'Connor was definitely rushing across the square towards The Curlew. For a second, Helen felt like locking the door in her face.

The woman saw them and came dashing up. 'Mr Moore, it's me. You remember my little dog, Oliver?'

Helen and Hannah stopped in their tracks.

'Yes. Why what's the matter?' David Moore went out on to the pavement.

'He's disappeared. I can't find him!'

The girls felt their hearts miss a beat. Scruffy . . . lost!

'What do you mean?' Their dad tried to calm her down. She looked pale and breathless, clutching her coat across her chest.

'I left him in the car to come to your meeting.'

'Did you park where we last saw you?'

She nodded. 'By Bassetts' shop. But when I went back, he'd gone!' She shook her head as if she still couldn't believe it. 'Vanished. No sign of him anywhere!'

'Come in and sit down.' Quietly Mary Moore led Miss O'Connor into the warmth. 'Let's think for a moment. What do you suppose could have happened? Was the car door locked, for instance?'

The woman sat down with a worried frown. 'Yes, I locked it. I'm sure I did. Why, you don't suppose he's been kidnapped?'

The twins' mum shook her head. 'It's unlikely. But if the door was definitely locked, was there any other way Oliver could have escaped?

Through a window, for instance?' She did her best to help Miss O'Connor calm down.

'Yes, he could have climbed out of a window.' Hannah knew what the puppy was like; a bundle of furry energy, never still, always up to mischief.

Miss O'Connor thought hard. 'I must have left the side window open to let fresh air into the car, but only a tiny crack.' She looked up helplessly. 'He wouldn't want to run away from me, would he?'

'I wouldn't blame him if he did,' Helen muttered under her breath. Her dad gave her a warning look.

'No, no, all puppies are naturally naughty,' Mary Moore soothed.

Hannah jumped in. 'The thing is, there's no point sitting here wondering how he got out, is there? What we should be doing is trying to find him!'

'Agreed!' David Moore reached for his jacket. 'I'll go,' he volunteered. 'Can you manage to close up and clear away by yourself here, Mary?'

She told him she could. 'Take Hannah and Helen,' she suggested.

'And Speckle.' Helen grabbed his lead.

Before they had time to think, they were all out in the square, breathing clouds of steam into the dark, cold air, their feet echoing over the cobbles as they headed for Miss O'Connor's empty car.

'Oliver!' Her voice rang out. 'Oliver, where are you?' She looked in every shop doorway, under the arches of the stone market building, down side streets that led off in all directions.

Helen held Speckle on the lead and let him follow his nose. He snuffled into shadowy corners, ran here and there, the white tip of his tail showing in the dark.

Meanwhile, Hannah went with her dad to inspect the empty silver car.

'This window is open,' she pointed out. 'But like she said, not enough for Scruffy to escape.'

'Scruffy?' He examined the door handle and found that it was unlocked.

'Our secret name for him,' she explained.

'That's funny.' Her dad fiddled with the door. 'This lock has been broken.' He peered into the car. 'I wonder if Miss O'Connor knows that her radio is missing,' he said, pointing to a bunch of coloured wires dangling out of the dashboard. 'Well I never! Better tell her the bad news, someone.'

So Hannah ran quickly to fetch her and show her.

Miss O'Connor's hand went up to her cheek and she gasped. 'Oh my goodness, it's been stolen. It wasn't like that when I left it!'

David Moore said this explained everything. 'The thief would break the lock and open the door to steal the radio. Scruf . . . Oliver would seize his chance, jump out and scarper. Of course, the thief wouldn't care, as long as the puppy didn't make a noise and give him away. He'd make a quick getaway, and that would be that.'

'But where would he go?' To Helen and Hannah's surprise, Miss O'Connor didn't seem too worried about her radio; only about her puppy. She turned to the twins. 'You two know the area. Have you got any idea where he would run to?'

'There are loads of side streets,' Hannah answered. 'He could have got lost down one of them and not be able to find his way back to the square.'

'Or he might have smelt some good smells coming from one of the houses and crept inside.' Helen knew how cheeky Scruffy could be.

'What if a door slammed shut on him and he can't get out?' Hannah pictured him trapped.

'Or else he ran on to a main road?' Helen's mind flew ahead. 'There's a really fast road out by the supermarket. The traffic would scare him and he wouldn't know what to do.'

Miss O'Connor's face went pale. She glanced here and there, unsure where to begin the search. 'Oh, the silly thing! Of course, it's my fault. I should have trained him to be sensible near cars!' she frowned. 'But I haven't had time to take him to classes. Yes, it's my fault if he panics and runs into the road.' She pictured the worst.

'Now, we don't know that any of these things have actually happened,' Mr Moore reminded them. He kept his feet firmly on the ground. 'So until we do find out for sure, let's all keep calm.' He asked Miss O'Connor if she had a torch in the car. She delved into the glove compartment and drew one out.

'You take this.' The twins' dad handled it to them and gave instructions. 'We'll split up. You two take this half of the square and all the side streets leading down to the lake. Take Speckle with you, then I know you'll be safe. Miss O'Connor and I will stick to the top half, and all the streets as far as the school and the church. Got that?'

Helen and Hannah nodded.

'If you find him, bring him back here to the car. We'll all meet up again in half an hour.' He turned up the collar of his jacket. 'Don't worry,' he told the anxious owner. 'Between us we're bound to find him!'

'Thank you!' She took a deep breath, then turned to Helen and Hannah. 'I mean it. I really am very grateful. Especially since I know what you must think of me!'

Hannah cleared her throat and stepped back, Helen stared at the ground. She fiddled with Speckle's lead.

Miss O'Connor hurried on. 'I know you girls

83

have heard me tell poor Oliver off so many times you must think I don't care about him.'

Hannah coughed again and shuffled. Helen switched to gazing up at the stars.

'Well, I wouldn't blame you if you were glad that Oliver has run away and thought it served me right. Only, believe me, I do care about him. When he's naughty and hard to control, I don't know what to do. Something comes over me and I get very cross with him. But I do love him all the same.' Her voice broke and she turned away.

'Off you go, girls,' their dad said quietly, pushing them gently away. 'And remember, be back here in half an hour, whatever happens.'

They nodded and set off down the street that ran by the side of Bassetts'. Helen held Speckle on the lead, while Hannah shone the torch down all the dark alleyways.

'Do you believe her?' Helen whispered, as soon as they were out of earshot. Her head was spinning with surprise. What if Miss O'Connor wasn't Cruella de Vil in disguise after all?

'About caring for Scruffy?' Hannah thought long and hard. She shone the torch amongst some dustbins, saw a cat's eyes glint and watched the cat slink away over a wall. 'I suppose so.' After all, how could anyone resist the puppy's cute hairy face and dark brown eyes?

'But that still doesn't make her a good owner,' she said firmly, setting off across the street and shining the yellow torch beam along the length of another cold, deserted alley.

Eight

'That's a good boy, Speckle!' Helen cried. She let him off the lead and he surged ahead, nose to the ground, tail wagging.

After twenty minutes of frantic searching, their dog had finally picked up a trail.

'Good boy, we know you can do it!' Hannah raced after him. Speckle was taking them down a street that led to the lake, stopping by a lamp-post to check the scent, padding in this direction, then that. At last he chose a new route and led them on.

He was going at a fast trot, leaving the houses

behind. When he came to the road that ran alongside the lake, he stopped at the kerb to wait for the twins.

Hannah and Helen arrived out of breath. A car cruised by, carrying a family Christmas tree on its roof-rack. Across the road the lake stretched for miles; a sheet of dark water sparkling between the steep mountains, fringed at the edges by a layer of hard, white ice.

'This is near where we first saw Scruffy!' Helen said, catching her breath and giving Speckle the order to cross.

Hannah recognised the clump of thick bushes where Miss O'Connor's car had been parked. Beyond them lay the stony beach and the dark, humped shape of the upturned boat. 'That's right. He must have found his way back here all by himself!' She felt a surge of hope as she followed Speckle on to the pebbles.

The dog sniffed here and there, fussed and hovered by the boat, then gave up and went to try elsewhere.

'That must have been Scruffy's old scent, from when he was trapped here before.' Helen had held her breath, but had to let it go with a sigh as Speckle backed off. So near, yet so far.

'Let's hope it hasn't been the old scent that he's been following all along,' Hannah said quietly, flashing the torch along the rim of the boat just to make sure. Speckle was right; there was no sign of the excitable little puppy.

She raised the beam and flashed it on to the lake, picking out large rocks fixed solid in the sheet of ice at the water's edge. Beyond that she could see thinner, clearer ice surrounding a small island with a tree and some low bushes. But, as for Scruffy, there wasn't a single clue.

'No, look, he's on to something!' Helen pointed to Speckle, who had gone off across the beach, nose to the ground, suddenly excited by a new trail. He reached the water's edge, turned and barked for them to follow.

Helen was quickest off the mark. But she joined him with a puzzled frown. 'What, Speckle? What have you found?' The beach seemed empty and silent.

He barked again, jerking his head towards the lake.

'There's nothing out there!' Helen said.

'Shh!' Hannah warned. She knew Speckle; how he was never wrong about picking up a scent. 'Listen for a second!'

Speckle reached out and put one foot on to the ice. His claws skidded and he pulled back.

'Stay!' Hannah ordered. She strained to pick up a more distant sound. 'Did you hear that?'

Helen nodded. 'A kind of scratching, pattering noise?'

There it was again; out on the ice, close to the small island.

Speckle barked and tried the ice again.

'Stay!' Hannah said sharply, afraid that he would put his full weight on to it. No one knew how thick it was, only that it was risky to set foot on it, just in case.

'I wish it wasn't so dark!' Helen hissed. 'Point the torch out there, Hannah.' The skidding noise was growing louder, then there was a movement, a pale shape out on the ice.

Hannah shone the beam towards the island. 'Please, no!' she whispered. It would be just like Scruffy to go playing where it wasn't safe. What did he know about thin ice and the freezing water underneath?

But it was true; there he was racing round the side of the island, skidding into view. The yellow beam picked out his light fawn coat; they heard him yelp as he slid out of control.

Hannah felt the torch wobble in her hand. She bit her lip, hoping and praying that the ice would bear the puppy's light weight.

'Slow down,' Helen called. The more he skidded and bounced up again, the more he rushed and grew excited to see them standing waiting at the water's edge, the more likely it was that the ice would give way. 'Come here, there's a good boy!' she coaxed.

Scruffy barked and bounded towards them. There was a crack, the white ice was split by a jagged, dark line.

Hannah screamed. 'Look out!'

The puppy lost his balance. One back leg slid over the edge of the jagged gap into the black water beneath.

'Oh no!' Helen's heart leapt into her mouth.

Scruffy struggled but only slid further off the

ice. Now both his back legs were gone, he was clinging on with his front paws, but the shattered ice was cracking and tilting, he was sliding again, until at last he lost his grip and splashed into the water. They could still see his head, struggling to stay on the surface. Then, with a terrified yelp and a splash, he was gone.

For a second Hannah and Helen stood numb. The torchlight flickered on the broken ice. Water sloshed between the fragments, wearing a larger hole.

'What now?' Helen groaned.

But there was no time to make a plan because Speckle made the decision for them. For the first time in his life, he disobeyed an instruction.

He saw Scruffy vanish, he heard the black water sloshing against the ice, and without a thought, without waiting for an order, he took the law into his own hands. He stepped out on to the ice.

'No, Speckle, come back!' Hannah cried, her voice terrified.

He ignored her. Surefootedly, keeping his eye on the dangerous hole ahead, he made his way to the spot where Scruffy had vanished.

Helen's heart almost stopped as she saw him inch forward. If only the ice would hold this time . . . !

Speckle pressed on carefully. Once, when the ice cracked beneath his feet, he paused. But Scruffy had been under the water for at least a minute. There was no time to lose.

'I can't bear this!' Hannah turned her head away. If their beloved Speckle fell through the ice after the puppy, her heart would break.

'It's OK, he's almost there!' Helen whispered. She took the torch from Hannah and shone it steadily so that Speckle could see where to tread.

Hannah steeled herself to look. There he was, balancing at the edge of the hole. And there, by a miracle, was Scruffy's head, bobbing to the surface and Speckle leaning out, grabbing him by the scruff of the neck with his strong teeth.

Hardly seeming to know where he was, the puppy struggled to hold his head above water. He let the bigger dog take his weight, went limp as Speckle dragged him, dripping and shivering out of the lake.

But the weight of two dogs together was too much for the fragile ice. The twins heard it crack again, saw it split. And this time Speckle went down with Scruffy, slipping and sliding as the ice tilted and sank, hanging on to him for dear life.

Nine

As Hannah cried aloud and Helen covered her eyes, Speckle struggled to stay afloat. He held Scruffy between his jaws and shouldered the broken ice aside, swimming strongly for the island.

'Go on, Speckle, you can do it!' The twins urged him on.

Speckle was a few metres from the island, only his head showing above water, still carrying Scruffy. He struggled past lumps of ice. Jagged slices veered towards him, he bobbed to one side and swam on.

'How's he going to haul himself on to dry land?' Hannah cried. They'd nearly made it, but Speckle's fight to save Scruffy wasn't over yet.

'Quickly!' Helen gasped. She was afraid that the freezing water would be too much, that Speckle wouldn't be able to drag himself and the puppy clear before they froze to death.

'He can't do it!'

Speckle had reached the island, but there was no way up on to dry land. Huge boulders stood between him and safety. He paddled frantically, looking for an easier slope.

'They're going to freeze!' Helen stood helpless, separated from the dogs by twenty metres of cracking, dangerous ice.

'Speckle, keep trying!' Hannah called. 'Don't give in now!'

He heard and swam around the boulders, disappearing for a few seconds, making their hearts sink.

Then he came back into view, still trailing Scruffy through the water, tiring now and sinking lower into the water.

'Oh, he's not going to make it!' Helen's voice

was small and scared. She could see him beginning to falter.

'Yes, he is!' Hannah insisted. 'Go on, Speckle!'

At last he came to a slope which he might be able to manage. He spotted it and swam at it with a last burst of energy. Then his feet touched dry land. In the dim light of the torch, they saw him haul himself out of the water, dragging Scruffy, determined not to let go. First two feet, then his long body, looking skinny and pathetic now that his coat was soaked against his skin, then his back legs, scrambling up the icy slope, slipping, recovering, standing at last.

'He did it!' Hannah and Helen hugged each other and cried. 'Speckle, you're brilliant!' they called across the frozen water.

Wearily Speckle let Scruffy fall to the ground. He stood and shook himself dry, bent his head to lick warmth back into the shivering pup. Then he lifted his head and looked at the twins, as if to say, 'Who said I couldn't make it?' A proud, pleased look, though he was weak with exhaustion.

'How are we going to get them off the island?'

Hannah asked. She was the first to come round and try to think clearly. 'We can't leave them there for very long. The temperature's way below freezing tonight, and they're both soaking wet. There's no way they can survive!'

Helen agreed. She looked round wildly for an answer to the problem. 'Couldn't we risk treading on the ice to fetch them?' she asked. There were areas where the ice was still unbroken. It looked solid enough if they were careful and picked out a pathway well away from the gaping holes.

'Too dangerous,' Hannah decided. 'One slip and we'd be in trouble.' Instead of two dogs to be rescued, there would be two dogs and two girls. 'No, there must be a better way.'

'The boat!' Helen cried. There it was, lying high and dry on the beach, turned upside down; just the thing for them to get across to the island. She ran towards it, flashing the torch across the pebbles.

'Stay there!' Hannah stopped to yell an order to Speckle. 'Look after Scruffy. Don't let him move!' Then she was racing after Helen, helping her to roll the heavy boat the right side up, beginning to tug and drag it towards the lake.

'At least there are oars inside!' Helen gasped. 'We'll have to pull together. We'll never get anywhere if we don't.'

'OK: one, two, three, pull!' Hannah and Helen heaved, the boat shifted a few inches before the muscles in their arms gave way and they ground to a halt.

'Take a break.' Helen slumped against the boat. 'Just a few seconds. Ready again? One, two, three, pull!'

Three times they did this, then four. Each time they edged closer to the water. But it was taking them a long time. In the dim distance they could see the two dogs on the island; Scruffy huddled on the frozen ground, Speckle standing over him.

'We've got to hurry!' Hannah insisted. 'They're going to die of cold!'

One last effort; more aching muscles and bursting lungs, the sound of the wooden hull scraping over the stones, and finally, to their relief, the crunch of breaking ice as the boat reached the water.

Then it was downhill, the boat slipping easily

and smashing through the layer of ice with the force of its own weight.

Now they must move fast. They hopped into the boat, seized the oars and used them as levers to push away from the shore. Meanwhile, the ice broke up under them and the boat floated free. They sat and began to row, steering towards the thin ice where Scruffy had fallen through, knowing that the boat would smash through, that they would be able to push and paddle and struggle their way towards the island where Speckle and Scruffy still waited.

'Hang on!' Helen told them. The island loomed near. They could see Speckle shivering, his grey flecked legs wobbling with weariness as he watched over Scruffy. The puppy seemed not to be moving now. He lay curled in a ball, his fur stuck to his sides, his whole body trembling.

They were a long way from the shore, smashing through the ice, when they heard shouts.

'Hannah, Helen! Come back!'

It was their dad, standing on the beach, waving his arms at them.

'For God's sake, come back!'

'We can't, Dad!' Helen strained at her oar. 'Speckle and Scruffy are stranded. We'll bring them back, but we'll need blankets and things. Can you go and get some help?'

In a flash he took in what was happening and went running back up the beach. But he left Miss O'Connor standing terrified, watching the boat struggle towards the island.

'Nearly there,' Hannah gasped. She felt her oar strike the rocks, heard the bottom of the boat grate against something more solid than ice. They shuddered to a halt.

Then they were both leaping out of the boat and running up the rocks, flinging themselves at Speckle and Scruffy, wrapping them in their coats and huddling them against the warmth of their own bodies.

'Oh, Speckle!' Helen cried. She held him close, so full of pride that she felt the tears well up. 'You're so brave!'

Hannah lifted Scruffy and hugged him to her. She was gentle as she wrapped her jacket around him, rubbing his back gently to make him warm, stroking his head and murmuring to him. 'There, you're safe now. We'll take you back with us. There's no need to worry any more.'

The puppy's eyes were closed. Only his head poked out from Hannah's jacket, with its bedraggled fringe of cream hair, its floppy grey ears. He lay limp and trembling.

Still down on her knees and hugging the hero of the hour, Helen looked up. 'We're not too late, are we?'

Hannah stroked Scruffy, willing him back to life. If, after all Speckle had done to save him, the puppy were to die . . . She looked across the expanse of ice to where Miss O'Connor stood.

'Is he still alive?' she shouted, her voice floating up strangely into the starry sky. 'Please tell me he's still alive!'

'He is, but only just!' Hannah called back. 'We're going to bring him and Speckle back across!'

Together she and Helen stumbled down the rocks towards the boat. Speckle managed to walk by himself, though his head hung low and he staggered as he climbed inside. But Hannah had to carry Scruffy, cradling him gently inside her padded jacket, settling him into the bottom of the boat beside the bigger dog.

'Does Speckle still need your jacket?' she asked Helen. The longer Scruffy's eyes stayed closed, the more worried she grew. Was he unconscious, she wondered. Was this the first sign of what happened when people and animals died of the cold?

Helen handed the spare jacket to her and Hannah tucked Scruffy inside it. 'Come here, Speckle,' she said. 'Lie down next to Scruffy.'

Speckle did as he was told on unsteady legs. He lay and curled himself around the bundle of jackets with Scruffy inside. Licking the puppy's face, he whimpered and settled his head next to his.

'OK, ready?' Helen pushed off from the island with her oar. They began the hard journey back to the shore, to the crunch of icy water and the anxious cries of Miss O'Connor.

'Watch out for the hidden rocks! Mind the jagged pieces of ice! You're steering too far to the left!' Her voice pierced the silence of the night.

The oars went splash into the black water, a sheet of ice glinted up at them as Hannah and Helen slowly worked their way to safety.

Ten

'It's touch and go,' David Moore said as he lifted Scruffy out of the boat and laid him on the beach. He stooped over Scruffy with a blanket from the cafe, ready to rub the puppy down and warm him up.

The twins' mum had run back with him, desperate to know that they were all safe. They'd arrived just in time to see Helen and Hannah reach the shore.

'Oh, wake up, Oliver!' Miss O'Connor cried, down on her hands and knees beside him.

The puppy lay on the pebbles with his eyes

still closed. Mr Moore put the blanket over him, rubbed him, then shook his head. 'I'm no expert, but he looks pretty far gone to me.'

'Don't say that,' Hannah's lungs hurt, her arms ached as she climbed, exhausted, out of the boat. Don't let it all have been for nothing!

'But you're all right?' Mary Moore helped Helen out of the boat. She threw her jacket around her shoulders.

'Yes. Let Scruffy keep the jacket. He needs it,' she protested, staggering on to the beach after Hannah.

'He's got the blanket now. Keep it on, Helen. I'm worried about you catching your death of cold!'

So she huddled inside her jacket, hovering over Scruffy.

'Where's Speckle?' Hannah asked. She too had her jacket around her shoulders. She was shaking and gasping for breath. 'Did he get out of the boat?'

'He's here.' David caught hold of the dog's collar and held him tight. 'That's right, boy, you're a good dog!'

Speckle pushed forward to see where Scruffy lay. He crept close to him, thrusting his nose against the puppy's face, whining and urging him to wake up.

'He's dead, isn't he?' Miss O'Connor wailed, her hand over her mouth, tears rolling down her pale cheeks.

But Speckle nosed at his little friend and licked his face with his rough tongue. He whimpered loudly, then licked again.

Scruffy's head jerked back.

'Did you see that?' Helen cried, clinging on to

her last shred of hope. 'He moved!'

'Are you sure?' Mary thought it might be Speckle's rough attempts to revive him that had pushed his head backwards.

'Yes. There; he did it again!'

'He licked his lips!' Hannah saw the little pink tongue slip out and curl up.

They craned forward to make sure. And yes; Scruffy was stirring. His head moved again, then at last he opened his eyes and gazed at Speckle.

Helen sank back. A wave of relief swept over her as she tilted her head and looked up at the stars. Hannah closed her eyes. Scruffy was going to be OK!

'Thank heavens!' Miss O'Connor whispered. She put out her hand to stroke the little dog's head. 'I can't thank you enough!' Tears still streamed down her face as she grasped hold of the twins' hands. 'I thought we'd lost him, I really did!'

'It's Speckle you should thank,' Hannah said. 'He risked his life.'

Their own dog had licked Scruffy's face until

he revived. He gave a yelp of encouragement. *That's better!*

Scruffy began to struggle free of the blanket. He was weak, but eager to be back on his feet. There was a dazed look in his eyes, he shook his head.

'Now, now, you'd better stay put under that nice warm blanket for a while.' David Moore tried to tuck him up again.

But Scruffy would have none of it. He fought to be free.

'OK.' The twins' dad let him do as he wished.

They all watched him stand and take his first wobbly step. Down he went, then he was up again, with Speckle by his side, nudging him back on to his feet, telling him he could do it if he tried.

'Brave little dog!' Miss O'Connor cried. She too got to her feet and wiped her face. 'See, he's not going to let himself be beaten!' She managed a smile as Scruffy wobbled then got up for a second and then a third time.

'He's up!' Mary Moore reported. 'No, he's not; he's down! No, he's up again!' Smiles broke out all around.

'Let's get back to the Curlew.' David thought it was time for them all to get warm. 'We'll be able to take a good look at Scruf . . . Oliver . . . there to see if we need to fetch the vet.'

Miss O'Connor nodded. 'Call him Scruffy if you like; I don't mind.'

'Shall you carry him, or shall I? He won't be strong enough to walk the whole way,' Mr Moore warned.

'Let one of the girls.'

Helen stepped forward to volunteer, then thought again. 'You do it,' she said to Hannah.

'No, it's OK, you do it.' Hannah was feeling equally generous.

They dithered on the freezing beach.

'Well, one of you decide!' Mary Moore laughed.

So they took it in turns, Hannah first, then Helen, to take Scruffy through the town, back to the warmth of the cafe.

When they got there, a small crowd had gathered for news of the daring rescue. Word had got round that the Moores had rushed down to the lake with blankets; something about the twins rowing out to rescue a couple of dogs. Now they waited to hear what had really happened.

'You will come in, won't you?' Mary Moore said kindly to Miss O'Connor.

Helen had handed the puppy back to his owner and everyone was dithering again; being polite, feeling awkward after all that had happened earlier in the afternoon.

'If it wouldn't be too much trouble,' the council officer said, hesitating in the doorway.

'No trouble at all.' The twins' mum went inside to make more coffee.

They followed into the bright room with its clean white tablecloths and glittering Christmas decorations. Miss O'Connor put Scruffy down and let Speckle fuss over him once more. 'You're very kind,' she said, relaxing, beginning to smile shyly. 'Too kind, considering what we plan to do to you after Christmas.'

Hannah heard and risked a sideways glance at Helen. Miss O'Connor was nowhere near as nasty as they'd thought. For a start, she actually cared about Scruffy!

Helen showed Hannah her secretly crossed fingers.

Meanwhile, Scruffy had dried off and was looking his old self; wild-haired and woolly. His whiskery face was perky, and he came up to Helen and Hannah with his enormous, appealing eyes. They smiled and made a fuss of him.

'Who was a naughty dog?' Helen cooed.

'Who ran away? Who gave us all a terrible fright?' Hannah pretended to be cross.

Miss O'Connor cleared her throat and reached for her mug of coffee. 'Of course, the council's plan isn't absolutely settled yet. That's to say, we haven't made any final decisions about the work on the square . . . especially in the light of the petition . . . we may well decide to hold another meeting before we give the go-ahead . . . that's to say . . . nothing's definite.'

'Meaning what?' Hannah whispered. Miss O'Connor was being as clear as mud!

'Shh!' Helen didn't know what she meant either, but she guessed by the twinkle in her dad's eyes that without actually saying so, Miss O'Connor had changed her mind!

'After all, it is Christmas!' Miss O'Connor went on, blushing as she spoke. 'The season of good will. And I do recognise the level of public opposition . . .'

'She means everyone's against it,' Helen whispered to Hannah.

'I know *that*!' Hannah retorted.

'In fact, I've been very impressed by the "Save Our Square!" campaign.'

Hannah gave Helen a thumbs-up sign.

'And I'll certainly reconsider the proposed improvements in the light of local concern . . .'

'What?' Helen whispered.

'Search me.' Hannah wished grown-ups would say what they meant.

'So there's hope?' Mary Moore came in with her commonsense voice. 'I can tell the other shopkeepers not to let it spoil their Christmas?'

Miss O'Connor blushed. 'Certainly there's hope.' She glanced at Helen and Hannah. 'In fact I would say, all things considered, there's a very good chance of the council changing its mind!'

'Yes!' Hannah punched the air.

'Yes!' Helen caught hold of Hannah and spun her round. Speckle and Scruffy began to bark and prance around the room.

For a second Mary Moore's eyes closed and she heaved a sigh. When she opened them again, Miss O'Connor was standing up, ready to leave.

'Quick, let's tell the others!' Hannah nipped outside with Helen on to the pavement. The news of Miss O'Connor's change of heart spread smiles all around. Peter Bassett hugged his wife, the Thomases praised the twins. 'If it hadn't been for you rescuing that little puppy of hers, we'd never have changed her mind!' they said. They all wanted to wait and thank the woman from the council when she came out.

So the twins went back in to see if she was ready. There she was shaking hands with their dad, holding Scruffy tucked under one arm. Their mum was smiling happily, wishing her a Merry Christmas. When the doorbell jangled, they turned to the girls with pleased, secret expressions.

'What's going on?' Hannah asked. 'Why are you smiling?'

'Me?' David Moore teased. 'I'm always smiling; you know that.'

'Come on, Mum, what's happened?' Helen

wanted to know why they were behaving like this, standing in a row, hugging a special secret to themselves. No one moved.

'What would you say if I told you that Father Christmas has just paid us an early visit?' David Moore asked. He shot a sideways look at Miss O'Connor.

' "Nonsense!" ' Their mum jumped in. Her mouth was twitching, her eyes sparkling. 'That's what you'd say!'

'Maybe,' Helen said slowly.

'It depends.' Hannah eyed them carefully. What on earth were they all up to?

'. . . That he came with a very wonderful present,' their dad went on. 'The best present in the world!'

Speckle sat at Miss O'Connor's feet, looking up at Scruffy. The puppy barked and wriggled in his mistress's arms.

Suddenly, at exactly the same moment, Helen and Hannah saw the light.

'You don't mean . . . !'

'You're not saying . . . !'

'. . . Scruffy!' they gasped.

Miss O'Connor stepped forward. No long speeches. No hard words. She held the puppy out to them. 'Please take him,' she said softly. 'I've thought about it and decided that this is definitely where he belongs.'

It was Christmas morning at Home Farm. The wind whistled through the horse chestnut tree outside Hannah and Helen's bedroom window. The twins had been awake since long before dawn.

'Now?' Helen whispered in the dark.

They'd waited and waited for it to get light. At last Hannah thought she'd spotted a tinge of pink in the sky. Now she was standing at the window, gazing out. 'Yes, now,' she said.

'Let's go!'

They slid their feet into their slippers, wrapped their matching blue dressing-gowns round them. Then they crept downstairs . . .

. . . to a mountain of presents stacked by the tree, to coloured lights and bunches of mistletoe and holly. And to Speckle, curled in his basket by the kitchen stove.

Hannah went over to give him his Christmas treat of doggie chocs. He heard her come in and opened one sleepy eye.

'And some for you,' Helen whispered to Scruffy.

The puppy was snuggled beside Speckle in the same basket. He smelt the chocolate and was suddenly up out of the basket, leaping and barking, chasing his tail and going mad for a taste of the treat. He skidded across the kitchen floor and scampered upstairs, straight on to Mary and David Moore's bed.

The twins' dad groaned and hid his head under the pillow. Mary Moore grabbed at the pup as it launched itself at her and gave her a hairy kiss.

It was five o'clock in the morning and Scruffy was making sure the whole house was awake.

The family looked at each other, the twins sitting on the edge of the bed, Scruffy bouncing on the duvet, Speckle sitting patiently on the floor. 'Happy Christmas!' They all said it together, hugging and kissing.

Speckle joined in with a bark. Scruffy escaped off the bed and charged around the room, ears

flopping, feet skidding, letting them know he was
there for good.

HOME FARM TWINS
Jenny Oldfield

66127 5	Speckle The Stray	£3.50	❏
66128 3	Sinbad The Runaway	£3.50	❏
66129 1	Solo The Homeless	£3.50	❏
66130 5	Susie The Orphan	£3.50	❏
66131 3	Spike The Tramp	£3.50	❏
66132 1	Snip and Snap The Truants	£3.50	❏
68990 0	Sunny The Hero	£3.50	❏
68991 9	Socks The Survivor	£3.50	❏
68992 7	Stevie The Rebel	£3.50	❏
68993 5	Samson The Giant	£3.50	❏

All Hodder Children's books are available at your local bookshop or newsagent, or can be ordered direct from the publisher. Just tick the titles you want and fill in the form below. Prices and availability subject to change without notice.

Hodder Children's Books, Cash Sales Department, Bookpoint, 39 Milton Park, Abingdon, OXON, OX14 4TD, UK. If you have a credit card you may order by telephone – (01235) 831700.

Please enclose a cheque or postal order made payable to Bookpoint Ltd to the value of the cover price and allow the following for postage and packing:
UK & BFPO – £1.00 for the first book, 50p for the second book, and 30p for each additional book ordered up to a maximum charge of £3.00.
OVERSEAS & EIRE – £2.00 for the first book, £1.00 for the second book, and 50p for each additional book.

Name ....

Address ....

....

....

If you would prefer to pay by credit card, please complete:
Please debit my Visa/Access/Diner's Card/American Express (delete as applicable) card no:

Signature ....

Expiry Date ....

ANIMAL ALERT
Jenny Oldfield

All Hodder Children's books are available at your local bookshop or newsagent, or can be ordered direct from the publisher. Just tick the titles you want and fill in the form below. Prices and availability subject to change without notice.

Hodder Children's Books, Cash Sales Department, Bookpoint, 39 Milton Park, Abingdon, OXON, OX14 4TD, UK. If you have a credit card you may order by telephone – (01235) 831700.

Please enclose a cheque or postal order made payable to Bookpoint Ltd to the value of the cover price and allow the following for postage and packing:
UK & BFPO – £1.00 for the first book, 50p for the second book, and 30p for each additional book ordered up to a maximum charge of £3.00.
OVERSEAS & EIRE – £2.00 for the first book, £1.00 for the second book, and 50p for each additional book.

Name ....

Address ....

....

....

If you would prefer to pay by credit card, please complete:
Please debit my Visa/Access/Diner's Card/American Express (delete as applicable) card no:

Signature ....

Expiry Date ....

ANIMAL ARK

Lucy Daniels

1	KITTENS IN THE KITCHEN	£3.50	☐
2	PONY IN THE PORCH	£3.50	☐
3	PUPPIES IN THE PANTRY	£3.50	☐
4	GOAT IN THE GARDEN	£3.50	☐
5	HEDGEHOGS IN THE HALL	£3.50	☐
6	BADGER IN THE BASEMENT	£3.50	☐
7	CUB IN THE CUPBOARD	£3.50	☐
8	PIGLET IN A PLAYPEN	£3.50	☐
9	OWL IN THE OFFICE	£3.50	☐
10	LAMB IN THE LAUNDRY	£3.50	☐
11	BUNNIES IN THE BATHROOM	£3.50	☐
12	DONKEY ON THE DOORSTEP	£3.50	☐
13	HAMSTER IN A HAMPER	£3.50	☐
14	GOOSE ON THE LOOSE	£3.50	☐
15	CALF IN THE COTTAGE	£3.50	☐
16	KOALA IN A CRISIS	£3.50	☐
17	WOMBAT IN THE WILD	£3.50	☐
18	ROO ON THE ROCK	£3.50	☐
19	SQUIRRELS IN THE SCHOOL	£3.50	☐
20	GUINEA-PIG IN THE GARAGE	£3.50	☐
21	FAWN IN THE FOREST	£3.50	☐
22	SHETLAND IN THE SHED	£3.50	☐
23	SWAN IN THE SWIM	£3.50	☐
24	LION BY THE LAKE	£3.50	☐
25	ELEPHANTS IN THE EAST	£3.50	☐
26	MONKEYS ON THE MOUNTAIN	£3.50	☐
27	DOG AT THE DOOR	£3.50	☐
	SHEEPDOG IN THE SNOW	£3.50	☐
	KITTEN IN THE COLD	£3.50	☐
	FOX IN THE FROST	£3.50	☐
	SEAL ON THE SHORE	£3.50	☐